Max the
Missing
Puppy

Max the Missing Puppy

by Holly Webb
Illustrated by Sophy Williams

For Rosie

tiger tales

5 River Road, Suite 128, Wilton, CT 06897
Published in the United States 2015
Originally published in Great Britain 2008
by Little Tiger Press
Text copyright © 2008 Holly Webb
Illustrations copyright © 2008 Sophy Williams
ISBN-13: 978-1-58925-467-1
ISBN-10: 1-58925-467-8
STP/1000/0057/1114

10 9 8 7 6 5 4 3 2 1

For more insight and activities, visit us at www.tigertalesbooks.com

Chapter One

Molly opened the gate, and stood holding it, waiting impatiently for her parents to catch up. "This is it!" she called. "Number 42!" She was sure she could hear squeaking and yapping from inside the house, and she couldn't wait to get inside.

At last her parents caught up. "Go and ring the bell, then!" said Molly's dad.

Molly heard the bell chime inside the house, and it was followed by an explosion of deep woofs. Then she heard paws thudding, and claws clicking, and something thumped into the door. Molly jumped back in surprise.

"Jackson, move! How can I open the door with you in front of it?" The voice didn't sound angry, more as though the dog's owner was trying not to laugh. "And the rest of you aren't helping!"

The deep barking had now been joined by a lot of squeaky little noises, all sounding very excited. The door opened, and a friendly-looking woman attempted to hold back a tide of black-and-white puppies as they swarmed around her feet. A huge, gray, shaggy dog was sitting beside her.

"Oh, good, you shut the gate. The puppies are a bit excited, I'm afraid, and they're desperate to get out and explore. I'm Sally Hughes, we spoke on the phone. Come on in!"

"I'm James Martin," Molly's dad said, picking up a puppy who'd managed to scramble over Mrs. Hughes's foot. "You spoke to my wife, Claire, on the phone, and this is our daughter, Molly. The dog-crazy one!"

They followed the excited puppies into the house. Molly looked at them in amazement. Mrs. Hughes had told her mom that there were six puppies, but surely there were more here. They seemed to be everywhere!

Mrs. Hughes led everyone into the kitchen. Another massive dog was stretched out, dozing on a comfy-looking cushion in the corner. Molly was sure she heard her groan as the puppies flooded back in and threw themselves all over her.

Mrs. Hughes smiled. "Poor Lady! I think she's actually looking forward to the puppies going to new homes. They're wearing her out!" She put cups of coffee down in front of Molly's mom and dad, and poured Molly a glass of juice.

Molly sipped from her glass, perched on the edge of her chair, wishing she could go and play with the puppies who were bouncing on their mom.

Mrs. Hughes noticed her hopeful eyes. "Go ahead and play with them! Just watch out for the puppies' dad,

Jackson. He's completely friendly, but he's huge, and if he wants to join in he can knock you over without meaning to!"

Molly knelt down on the floor, and the puppies looked at her with interest. The bravest of them started to creep slowly over to her, tail wagging gently. Molly stretched out a hand hopefully, and he butted it with his soft little head, then darted back. Molly thought he looked almost as though he was giggling!

"Mrs. Hughes?" she asked. "Why don't the puppies look like Jackson and Lady? They've got short fur, and they're black-and-white, but their parents are gray."

"That's the way it is with Old English sheepdogs," Mrs. Hughes said.

"They're born with that short, springy, black-and-white fur, and when it grows longer, it gets much lighter."

Dad was looking at Lady, her long fur glossy and smooth as it trailed over her cushion. "Grooming is going to be a lot of work."

Mrs. Hughes nodded seriously. "Yes, it really is. You have to make sure their coats are clean, and that they don't have any sore spots under all that fur. And they need a *lot* of exercise. Old English sheepdogs are a big commitment. I mean, no dogs are easy to take care of, but these can be hard work."

Molly looked up at her parents. It sounded scary, but she still wanted to take one of the puppies home!

Her mom looked doubtful. "Maybe this isn't a good idea since we've never had a dog before. Maybe a smaller dog would be better...."

The bravest puppy, who had a mostly white face, cute black ears, and a pirate-style eye patch, was creeping up to Molly again. This time he jumped up so his paws were on her lap, and he gave her a quick little lick.

Molly gasped delightedly. She'd been listening to her mom and hadn't noticed him. She tickled him under the chin. "I don't mind hard work," she said earnestly.

Another puppy, who had just the same adorable pirate look, bounded over and jumped into Molly's lap. Then he sat with his tongue hanging out, looking very pleased with himself.

Mrs. Hughes smiled. "It's not all work. They're incredibly affectionate dogs, and very good with children. Your daughter will have a friend for life." She crouched down next to Molly. "Those two are the boy puppies. They get into everything. The girls are a little bit more shy."

But now that their brothers had proven that this girl wasn't scary, the other puppies came crowding around to be petted, too. Soon Molly was covered in a black-and-white puppy blanket. She saw Lady watching her, one big dark eye peering out from behind her beautiful long fringe. The big dog sighed happily, and Molly was sure she was glad that someone else was being climbed on for once.

Molly's parents had been talking quietly. Molly tried to listen, but the puppies kept licking her ears, which made it difficult to hear. She hoped they hadn't changed their minds! When they'd seen the ad in the paper saying *Puppies for Sale*, and read that the house was only half an hour's drive away, it had seemed so perfect. It had taken forever to convince Mom and Dad that she was old enough to have a dog. They'd been saying "When you're older" for years! Molly didn't think she could bear it if she had to wait any longer. These puppies were so adorable. Molly could just imagine running along the beach after school every day with a huge, silver-furred dog like Jackson galloping beside her.

At last Dad came over and squatted down next to the puppies, too. Molly and all the puppies stared at him. Then one of the bouncy boy puppies leaned over and nudged him with his furry head, looking at him with twinkly, dark eyes.

Dad gently picked up the puppy and smiled at Molly. "So, do you think you can manage to keep one of these little rascals exercised?" he asked.

Molly gasped in delight. "You mean yes? We can have one?" She wrapped her arms around the other boy puppy, who was trying to burrow under her shirt.

"Yes. But you'll have to take care of the puppy, Molly. And it won't be a puppy for that long, either – soon it will be a great big dog the size of Lady and Jackson over there." Dad tickled the puppy, who wriggled happily. Then he looked down at the puppies romping all around them. "Now we just have to choose one…."

One!

Molly knew she should be excited about having a puppy at all, but she hadn't imagined how difficult it would be to pick just one. The puppies were all so sweet, and she wanted to take all of them home! How could she choose one – when it meant leaving all the others behind?

The two boys were fighting over a chew-toy now, pulling it back and forth with pretend fierce growls. The fight looked even funnier because they were so alike, the same size and with almost identical markings. The only noticeable difference was that their eye patches were on the opposite eyes – sitting side by side, they were like mirror images.

"You like them, don't you, Molly?" Mom asked, watching and laughing as one of the puppies let go, leaving his brother rolling onto his bottom, still clutching the toy. "Should we take one of the boys?"

"Oh, yes, they're really sweet. But how are we going to choose just one of them?" Molly stretched out her fingers to the puppies, who came over at once to sniff and lick them. She tickled the puppies behind their ears and hugged them as they climbed up into her lap. "Couldn't we...?"

"Only one puppy, Molly!" Mom said firmly. "One dog is quite enough."

Dad was nodding, too, and Molly sighed and looked at the puppies. Just then, the puppy with the right eye patch went to join his sisters, who were taking turns hanging off their mom's ears.

The other puppy watched them for a minute, then turned and gazed up at Molly, his tongue hanging out a bit so he looked goofy. Molly giggled. "Okay," she said, lifting him gently under his front legs, and snuggling him up against her shoulder. "Please can we have this one? He's really friendly and cuddly."

Mom leaned over to pet him. "He definitely is adorable. What are we going to call him?"

Molly gave the puppy a thoughtful look as he slobbered into her shoulder. "I think we should call him Max!"

Chapter Two

A week later, Molly and her parents were able to take Max home. He was eight weeks old now, and ready to leave his mother. Two of his sisters were about to go to new homes, too, and Mrs. Hughes said she was sure the others would find owners soon.

Molly still wished they could have Max's brother as well; they were such a pair that Molly hated to split them up. Then Max spotted Molly, flung himself at her, and nearly knocked her over, and Molly thought that maybe *two* dogs doing that all the time might be a bit much. But she was so happy that he remembered her!

"Hmmm. We're going to have to take him to a good puppy-training class," Molly's mom said. "It won't be long before he's big enough to hurt someone by accident. We need to be able to get him to calm down."

Mrs. Hughes was nodding. "I can recommend a local trainer. Max has just had his first shots, so you can take him to classes in a couple of weeks when he's had the second set. It's good to start young."

It was very exciting taking Max home. Mom and Dad had already spent quite a while putting a dog gate in the back of the car so that Max had his own special place to ride. Mom had to keep telling Molly to sit still, as she just couldn't help twisting around in her seat to check that Max was okay, all on his own back there.

At the house there was his new basket, his food bowl, and his leash for walks. Mrs. Hughes had said to introduce him to outdoor walks gently, as he was only used to quick runs in her garden. Molly was really looking forward to taking him for walks on the beach, but they needed to wait until after Max's booster vaccinations.

Meanwhile, Max was enjoying settling in at his new home. He did miss his brother and sisters, but Molly was a new and interesting person to play with, and he had her all to himself. He didn't have to share his toys either, and there were plenty! Molly had spent all her money on tennis balls and a nylon bone that would be good for Max's new teeth. They had a wonderful afternoon playing games. Max ran around so much he fell asleep in the middle of a game that they'd invented. All of a sudden, he had stopped bouncing, and when Molly had peered worriedly under the blanket to check that he was all

right, she had found him stretched
out with his nose between his paws,
fast asleep.

Molly had begged for Max to be allowed to sleep in her room, but Mom and Dad said no. They knew Max would end up on Molly's bed and not in his basket, even though Molly promised he wouldn't. "It's nice having a puppy on your bed, Molly," Mom explained, "but once Max is his full size, there'd be no room in your bed for you! You can't let him get on your bed now and then change your mind when he's bigger. He wouldn't understand."

So Max had to stay downstairs. Molly had given him her old teddy bear to snuggle up to, and a hot-water bottle, so he'd feel like he was curled up next to his mom, but it wasn't the same. After all the cuddles, Max just didn't understand why he was suddenly all on his own. He yapped hopefully, expecting someone to come back and play with him, but no one came. He got up, and pattered around the kitchen sniffing, trying to figure out where they all were. Earlier, Molly had played a game where she popped out from behind chairs at him – maybe this was the same? But she wasn't behind any of the chairs.

Max trailed back to his basket with his tail hanging sadly. Where had they all gone? Were they going to come back? He snuffled and whimpered to himself for a little while, then the exhausting day caught up with him again, and he fell asleep, burrowed into his blanket.

Upstairs Molly listened worriedly. It was so horrible hearing him cry, but Mom and Dad had explained that it would only upset Max more if she went down and then left him again. Her bedroom door was open, and she could hear the noises from the kitchen. She crept out very quietly, and leaned over the banister. He sounded so sad! But he was definitely getting quieter, so maybe he was going to sleep. Molly was tired, too, so she sat down on the top step, leaning against the wall, and tried not to let her eyes close.

Molly's parents had been watching TV in the living room. When they came upstairs a couple of hours later, Molly was fast asleep on the top step.

"Max…," she muttered sleepily, as her dad picked her up.

"He's fast asleep in his basket, Molly. Don't worry. Go to sleep."

The weekend just flew by. At school on Monday, everyone was envious when Molly told them about Max. She had a couple of photos that Dad had printed out for her, and she showed them off proudly.

"Oh, he's beautiful, Molly! My brother has an Old English sheepdog. They make great pets." Mrs. Ford, Molly's teacher, looked at the photo admiringly in the playground before school. "You should show those to the class when we do weekend news."

Molly didn't normally like the class news sessions that much, as she never felt like she had anything very exciting to say! But today she couldn't wait to tell everyone about her puppy. It was nice to have them all admiring Max's picture, too, because she was really missing him. She couldn't help wondering what he was doing, and if he was missing her, too. Mom had promised to play with Max, but she'd be busy doing stuff on the computer, too, as she worked from home. Molly hoped Mom wouldn't get too busy and forget about him.

Molly's school was really close to her house, so she walked there with her mom, and they picked up her friend Amy on the way. Then Amy's mom brought them home. That Monday Molly hurried Amy all the way back to their road, and then she raced home and flung herself through the front door.

Max jumped up and shot out of the kitchen to greet her. He'd been curled up in his basket, half-dozing, and wishing someone would play with him. He loved his new house, but it got very quiet without Molly there. Molly's mom had tried her best, but she just wasn't the same. With Molly he didn't have to stand there holding his bone and looking hopeful; she *knew* when he wanted to play. He danced around her, barking excitedly. When she swept him up for a hug he did his best to lick her all over, wanting her to know how much he'd longed for her to come home.

"Ooooh, stop, Max, not my ears! You're really tickling!" Molly held him out at arm's length and laughed at him.

"I don't need a bath. Did you have a nice day? Was he okay, Mom? Did he behave himself?"

Her mom was leaning on the doorframe and laughing. "Yes, but I think he really missed you. He looked all around the house several times, and he sat by the front door for quite a while. Why don't you take him in the yard? I took him out quickly at lunchtime, but I'm sure he'd like to go out again."

Max seemed to understand what "yard" meant. He dashed to the door, and jumped up and down, squeaking.

Molly giggled. "No, I think I need a rest after school ... it's okay, Max, I'm teasing! Come on, silly." She grabbed his squeaky ball and opened the door, letting Max streak out in a black-and-white blur.

He loved to be outside!

Max didn't stop missing Molly while she was at school – and she seemed to have to go to school all the time! He spent lots of time sniffing around for her, and he figured out that he could sneakily climb on to the back of the sofa to look out the window and see if she was coming. He got in trouble if Molly's mom caught him doing that, though.

Max was sure that if he could get outside, he could find Molly and be with her. He knew she missed him, too, and didn't understand why she went out without him. It had only taken him a few days of being in the house without her to explore everywhere inside. By the fifth day of Molly being at school, Max was very bored.

"We'll do lots of playing in the yard this weekend, Max," Molly promised as she got ready to leave for school on Friday morning. "I really wish we could go on the beach and show you the ocean, but Mrs. Hughes said you'll have to wait until about a week after your second vaccinations."

"He'd probably only try and eat the sand," Mom said, looking at Max's food bowl. It was empty, as usual, and polished sparkly-clean. "That dog is always hungry." She scratched him under the chin to show she wasn't really angry, and Max closed his eyes happily. Under the chin was his absolute favorite place to be tickled, and Mom and Molly sounded happy and excited. Everything was good.

Except Molly was about to go! Not again. Max gave a mournful little howl.

"I know, I'm sorry. But I'll be back this afternoon, and then we've got the whole weekend. And it's vacation! I'd almost forgotten! Nine days of no school. We'll spend lots of time outside. It's going to be great." Molly kissed the top of his head, and followed Mom outside, leaving Max staring sadly at the door.

Molly's mom was very busy that day. She kept shooing Max away when he tried to play. She did take him for a couple of little runs in the yard, but she wanted to go back in long before he did. By the middle of the afternoon, Max was missing Molly. It was a hot, sleepy day, even though it was only May, and being stuck in the house was making Max restless. Maybe Molly's mom was ready to play again. He brought his squeaky bone to her for a game, but she said, "Not now, Max," in a really firm voice, so he went and lay down in his basket, feeling bored. He rested his chin on the edge of the basket and sighed.

Maybe he should just sleep, and see if Molly's mom wanted to play later. His eyes were slowly closing when something fluttered past his nose. Max opened one eye to see a large butterfly swooping around his head. Surprised, he jumped up and barked furiously. What was it?

Mom dashed in, looking worried. Then she laughed. "Oh, Max, it's all right, it's only a butterfly. We'll get him out. You've probably never seen one before."

The butterfly was in no hurry to leave. Mom tried to waft it toward the kitchen window where it had come in, but it fluttered off into the living room and eventually settled on the curtains. Mom opened the window and after a couple of failed attempts, she scooped it out with a magazine.

"There," she said, soothingly, putting the magazine back on the coffee table. "It's gone now. Oh, look, Molly will be home soon. I need to finish that last little bit of work."

She went back to the computer in her office down the hall.

Max pricked up his ears when Mom mentioned Molly. Was she coming? He looked hopefully at the front door, but no Molly appeared. Disappointed, he wandered back into the living room and scrambled up on to the sofa so that he could look out the window and wait for her.

Then he noticed that Mom had left the window open.

Max jumped up, and stuck his head out the window, his nose quivering with excitement.

Now he could go and find Molly!

Molly dashed down the road from Amy's house, calling a quick good-bye over her shoulder. She went in the front door, expecting Max to be there leaping around her feet. But the house was strangely quiet. Max must be asleep.

Molly headed quietly into the kitchen, not wanting to wake him. He was so cute when he was asleep. Max's basket was empty, and she looked around, confused. Maybe he was with Mom in her office?

Feeling a little anxious, Molly walked quickly back into the hallway and opened the office door.

Her mom looked up with a start. "Molly! I'm sorry, I didn't hear you. I've been desperately trying to get this finished before the holiday. Did you have a nice day?"

"Yes – but Mom, where's Max?"

Mom looked down at Molly's feet as though she expected to see Max there. "Isn't he in his basket? I thought he was sleeping."

"No, I can't find him anywhere," Molly said. "He always comes running when I get home from school."

"He probably got himself shut in somewhere," said Mom, but she didn't sound as sure as Molly would have liked. She got up and together they went through every room in the house, calling to Max. Every time they opened a door, Molly hoped she'd hear a little patter of paws, and wild yapping, but there was nothing.

No Max.

They went back through every room, urgently this time, searching under all the beds in case he'd gotten himself stuck, opening cupboards, Molly frantically calling.

Still nothing.

Back downstairs, Mom was starting to look really worried, too. She stood in the living room, trying to think. "I took him in the yard after lunch, but he definitely came back in with me. Then I was working…. Oh! that butterfly surprised him. It flew in through the kitchen window," she explained. "He didn't know what it was. I let it out the window in here…." She did a slow turn toward the window, and her hand went to her mouth in horror. The window was still propped open. Definitely wide enough for a little dog to fit through.

Chapter Three

Meanwhile, Max was trotting along the pavement, sniffing enthusiastically. He knew he could find Molly. He'd know her smell anywhere! He had wriggled out the window quite easily, and fallen into the flower bed, but it didn't matter. Molly was going to be so pleased to see him! Only – he had been expecting to find her by now.

Molly's house was on the edge of the town, and although Max didn't know it, he was going completely the wrong way, heading out of town and away from the school where Molly had been. He had taken a few turns that looked interesting, passing some more houses like Molly's. Instinctively he'd avoided crossing any roads. The town was very quiet, but a few cars did come past, and he'd been scared. He shrank back against the fences and hedges as he heard the cars coming, roaring things that he sensed were dangerous. He kept hidden against the hedges, and no one saw him. Now he was heading along the road that led to Springfield, a small town several miles away. It was so nice to be outside, and he trotted along happily for a while, covering a big distance for such a small dog. He would see Molly soon, he was sure.

Eventually he came across an interesting-looking sloping path leading off the pavement. It was rough and stony, with sweet-smelling plants on either side. Max plunged down, eager to explore. The path led gently down to a beach, not the main beach where all the vacationers came, but a small rocky cove without much sand that was cut off at high tide. Max stopped short as he got his first sight of the ocean. The waves made a swooshing sound as they rushed in and out over the pebbles. He had a feeling that this wasn't where he'd find Molly, but it looked so exciting that he had to go and investigate.

He skittered down the rest of the path, scrambling over the stones, and stood on the beach, sniffing the salty smell of the ocean. It moved, and made a noise – was it alive? He went closer, ears pricked, ready to run if he needed to. Suddenly, a wave swept in and soaked his paws. Max yelped and jumped backward. It was cold!

Max stood back from the water and barked angrily at the ocean. It didn't seem to be listening, just sweeping in again and hissing at his feet. Max looked at it with his head to one side. Maybe it was playing a game. Perhaps it wanted him to chase it? He tried, dashing forward as the waves rolled back, then yapping excitedly as it chased him. It was a great game! And the ocean didn't get tired and say it needed to sit down, like Molly and her mom. Max played for a long time.

Then a chilly wind blew up, ruffling the surface of the ocean, and Max shivered. Suddenly, he realized how hungry he was. Molly would be home by now, and wondering where he was. Max whirled around and scrambled back up the path as quickly as he could. But when he got to the top, he looked around. Which way was home from here? He couldn't remember which way he'd come – he hadn't been thinking about having to go *back*.

Anxiously, Max sniffed the air, hoping to pick up a familiar smell to tell him which way to go. Nothing. No smell of home, or Molly. Max sat down at the top of the path, huddling close to the sign that said *To the Ocean*.

No one was around; just empty road stretching out in both directions. Seagulls were crying, but that was the only sound. Max whined miserably. He was lost.

Suddenly, a low buzzing sound rose in the distance, quickly getting louder. Max looked around, and cowered back against the sign as a car shot by, engine roaring, and vanished down the road. He had to move. He needed to find Molly, and get away from noisy monsters like that. Determined, he trotted a few steps down the road. He wasn't sure if it was the right way, but he had to go *somewhere*.

The road seemed to go on forever. Max was starving – he was used to several small meals of his special puppy food every day, and it felt like he'd missed at least three of them.

As he continued on, his paws started to hurt, too, because he'd never walked so far before. And it was getting harder to see, the daylight leaving a strange half-dusk that made shapes loom up at him. All the trees seemed to be waving big, scary branches at him, and the seagulls' cries suddenly sounded eerie.

Max stopped to rest, hiding in between some clumps of grass at the side of the road. He'd gone a long way out of town by now, and the road didn't have pavement anymore, just grassy banks on either side. Things were scurrying in the hedges behind him, and more and more Max wished he'd never left his warm, comfortable, *safe* house behind.

He pushed on, determined to find his way home. It suddenly seemed to have gotten much darker, and Max was so tired and confused that he started to wander along in the middle of the road, his legs shaking with weariness. But he refused to give up.

Another low buzzing noise; this time he felt it in his paws before he heard it. A car! Max looked around, frightened and confused by the bright lights that were racing up behind him. He tried to get out of the way, but he didn't know which way to go, and he wavered disastrously in its path. The driver didn't even see him.

The car caught him with the edge of its front bumper, and Max was thrown clear, landing in the hedges. He lay unconscious in the long grass, his leg bleeding.

When Molly's dad got home from work, the house was empty, but he could hear Molly's voice calling from the yard.

"Max! Max, where are you?" Molly sounded upset, and her dad dropped his bag in the hall and hurried out to see what was going on.

"Did Max get out?" he asked anxiously. "He didn't wriggle under the fence, did he? I thought that gap was too small."

Molly shook her head. Her eyes were

full of tears, and she gave her dad a hug, burying her face in his coat. She didn't want to be the one to tell him.

Molly's mom came down the side path around the house. "Oh, James, you're back!" She was feeling so guilty about accidentally letting Max out, and she kept telling Molly how sorry she was. "I left the front window open, and Max got out. We've been up and down the street, but we can't find him anywhere."

Molly was trying hard to forgive her mom, because she knew she hadn't meant to leave the window open, but it was difficult.

"There's just no sign of him," Mom said, close to tears. "I've spoken to all the neighbors, and no one has seen him.

But they've all promised to keep an eye out for him."

"If only he'd had his collar on," Molly said miserably. They'd bought Max a collar, but he hadn't been wearing it. He hadn't needed it on when he was only in the house and yard. They'd also been planning to take Max to the vet to get his next vaccinations, and the vet was going to put a microchip in his neck. It would have meant that if he got lost, any vet could check the chip and would know who he belonged to. They'd made an appointment for it to be done next week. They were taking him to the vet where Mrs. Hughes brought her dogs. It was a half-hour drive away, but Mrs. Hughes had said they were really good. The thought made Molly's eyes fill with tears. Who knew where Max would be by then?

That night, Molly went to bed worn out from searching up and down her street, and around the town, and cried herself to sleep. But a hundred miles away, another girl lay awake, too excited to close her eyes. In the corner of Jasmine's bedroom was a small suitcase, already packed. She knew she should go to sleep, since they were going to get up at six, and Dad wanted to be on the road by six-thirty, but she just couldn't stop thinking about how exciting it was to be going on vacation. And to the beach! It was only May, so it wouldn't be very hot, but she could put her feet in the water, and build sandcastles, and eat tons and tons of ice cream! It was going to be fantastic.

Jasmine must have fallen asleep eventually, because the next thing she knew, her mom was shaking her awake. For once she didn't have to be told to get up quickly; she was downstairs five minutes later.

"I'm too excited for breakfast," said Jasmine, when her mother offered toast.

"You need to eat something. It's going to take us all morning to get there," her dad said. He was drinking a cup of coffee and looking at the map. "Okay. So we get off the highway, and then once we get to Springfield, the nearest town, we keep going along the cliff road, but we have to make sure we watch for the sign for the cottage. The cottage owners said that if we get to Athens, a town about five miles further on, then we have to turn around because we've missed it! Okay, I'm going to put the bags in the car." He ruffled Jasmine's hair as he went past. "Don't worry, Jasmine. We'll be on the beach this afternoon!"

Max was still lying huddled under the hedges, his leg throbbing with pain. He felt weak and dizzy, and he couldn't stand up. He was so scared. What was going to happen to him? Molly had no idea where he was – he didn't even know where he was.

He still wasn't really sure what had happened, either. He'd been wearily wandering along the road, then those enormous lights had swept over him, and something hit him. Then he didn't remember any more. He wanted Molly. With a sad little snuffling noise, he laid his head down on his front paws. He couldn't move – he'd tried and his leg wasn't working. All he could do was wait, and hope. Maybe Molly would come looking for him. She wouldn't give up on him, would she?

Chapter Four

Jasmine bounced excitedly around the vacation cottage, racing in and out of all the rooms, and getting under Mom and Dad's feet.

"Can we go out and have a look around? Can we go and see the ocean?" she kept asking.

"After we've unloaded the car, I promise," her mom said, as she unpacked all the food they'd brought and stored it in the cupboards.

Jasmine sighed, and perched herself on the windowsill to stare out. The little cottage was right on the cliff, with only a tiny patch of grass separating it from a huge drop to the ocean. Mom and Dad had already made her promise to stay away from the edge. She had a beautiful view from there. The sun was sparkling on the water, and a couple of small boats were creeping past. The cottage was outside a town called Springfield. If they walked one way they'd get to the town, which had interesting-looking shops, and if they went the other way, they'd reach one of the many little paths down to the beach. Jasmine had been thinking that they should go and investigate the shops first, and maybe buy an ice-cream cone, but the shining water was calling to her, and now she definitely wanted to find the path down the cliff.

At last her parents had finished the unpacking and they were ready to go and explore.

"Shall we go and get an ice-cream cone?" her dad suggested. "I'd love something cool after lugging all those bags around."

"Oh, please can we go and look at the beach first?" Jasmine begged. "And can we go for a boat ride? The ocean looks so pretty out the window, really blue, with little waves. Pleeeaase!"

"I don't believe it. You're turning down ice cream?" Jasmine's mom said, laughing.

Jasmine looked thoughtful. "Well, I'm not saying I don't *want* one...."

Her dad grinned. "I'm sure we can do both. Let's take a quick look at the ocean, and then head into town."

Eagerly they set off along the road. It had a real vacation feel, not like the streets Jasmine was used to at home. This road had steep banks, and hedges full of wild flowers, and every so often something scuttled into the undergrowth as they passed. Just a little ways down from the cottage, a small white-painted sign pointing the other way said *Springfield 2 miles.* Jasmine walked ahead, looking excitedly for a path down to the ocean. "Oh, look! Here it is!" she called back, waving to her parents to catch up.

Suddenly, there was a strange little scuffling noise in the grass on the bank, and Jasmine jumped back. "Ugh! I hope it isn't a rat!" she said nervously to herself. But the scuffling was followed by a tiny whimpering sound. That definitely wasn't a rat. It sounded more like a dog....

Max had heard Jasmine calling, and for one hopeful moment he had thought it was Molly. He realized it wasn't her; this girl didn't smell right, but maybe she would help him anyway. He struggled to get up, but he couldn't. His leg hurt so much, so he just called out to her. *Please! Help me!* he whimpered.

Jasmine crouched down cautiously to peer into the grass, and saw Max's black eyes staring back at her, glazed and dull with pain. He thumped his tail wearily to show he was glad to see her.

"Oh, wow, aren't you beautiful! What are you doing here, puppy? Are you lost?" Then Jasmine saw his leg and gasped. She jumped up. "Mom! Dad! Come here, quick!"

Her parents had been strolling along, enjoying the early summer sunshine. Jasmine's anxious voice jerked them out of their daydream.

"What is it?" her dad asked, rushing up to her.

"It's a dog, a puppy, I mean. He's hurt! Oh, Dad, look at his leg...." Jasmine's voice faltered. Max's leg was badly cut and had bled a lot all over his white fur. "What are we going to do?"

"He must have been hit by a car," said Dad. "Poor little thing." He turned to

Jasmine's mom, who'd come running after them. "Did you see a vet in Springfield as we drove through?"

Jasmine's mom shook her head. "I'm not sure, but I think there would be. Is the little dog hurt?" she asked worriedly.

"Hit by a car, I think. We can't leave him here." He looked down at Max. "I wonder when it happened. He looks pretty weak."

Jasmine's mom nodded. "You and Jasmine stay here, and I'll go get the car, and some towels or something to wrap him in. Then we can drive him into Springfield and ask someone about a vet."

"Please hurry, Mom!" Jasmine gulped. The puppy looked so weak and sick lying in the grass. "Do you think it would be okay to pick him up?" she asked. "He looks so sad."

Dad shook his head. "I don't think we should move him more than we have to. His leg might be broken, or he might have other injuries we don't know about. And if he's really hurting, he might bite you, Jasmine."

Jasmine shook her head. "I'm sure he wouldn't. He looks such a nice little dog."

Max whined again, and stretched his neck to get closer to Jasmine. She wasn't his Molly, but he could tell she was kind and friendly.

Very gently, trying not to frighten him, Jasmine put her hand out for Max to sniff.

Max licked her hand a little, then exhausted by even such a tiny effort, he slumped back.

"Oh, no. I wish Mom would hurry with the car." Jasmine looked around anxiously, then spotted their car coming along the road.

"How's he doing?" her mom asked as she jumped out, grabbing a pile of towels.

Jasmine's eyes were full of tears as she answered. "He's getting weaker. We have to hurry."

The vet's receptionist looked up as they barged through the door. "Oh, I'm sorry, we're actually just about to close—" Then she saw the puppy huddled in a towel in Jasmine's arms, and the blood seeping through the pale pink fabric. "Bring him in! This way. Mike, we've got an emergency," she called as she held open a door for Jasmine and her parents.

A tall, young man in a white jacket was looking at a computer screen inside the room, which was very clean and shiny, and smelled of disinfectant. He swung around quickly, his eyes going to the towel-wrapped bundle.

Jasmine just held Max out to him, not saying anything. She didn't know what to say, and the relief of finally getting to the vet, where someone might be able to help the poor little dog, was making her feel choked with tears.

The vet took Max and laid him carefully on the table. Max's eyes were closed, and he wasn't moving. Jasmine knew he was still alive, because she'd been watching him breathing, but even that seemed to have gotten weaker in the last few minutes.

The vet started gently checking Max over. "What happened?" he asked, without looking up.

"We don't know," Jasmine whispered. "We found him."

"We're here on vacation," her dad explained. "We were out for a walk, and Jasmine heard him crying. We guessed he'd been hit by a car."

The vet nodded. "He's very lucky. If he'd been out there much longer I don't think he would have made it. As it is," he looked up at Jasmine, "I can't promise that he will, but he's got a chance. His leg isn't broken, just badly cut, but he's lost a lot of blood, and he's very weak. I'm going to sedate him and put him on a drip, then stitch up the cut. If he turns the corner in the next couple of hours, he should be okay. But he's young, and that amount of blood loss in such a small dog…." He trailed off, but they all knew what he meant.

Jasmine gulped. "Can we wait while you do it? That would be okay, wouldn't it?" she asked her parents.

The vet smiled sympathetically at her. "Of course. You can stay in the waiting room." He was already gently gathering Max up to take him to the operating room. The puppy looked so small and helpless, and Jasmine just couldn't hold back the tears that were starting to trickle down the side of her nose.

Her mom hugged her gently, and led her out to the waiting room – and that was all they could do, just wait.

When the vet came back out into the reception area he was looking cautiously pleased. Jasmine had been leaning against her mom's shoulder, feeling worn out from her excitement and panic at finding the hurt puppy. But she jumped up immediately. "Is he going to be okay?"

The vet nodded slowly. "I think so. He's certainly got a good chance. The cut on his leg should heal well now that it's stitched, and except from that he's just bruised. Definitely no fractures. He really was lucky. He's just sleeping off the anesthetic now." He smiled down at Jasmine. "Would you like to see him?"

"Yes, please!" Jasmine nodded, and they followed the vet to a room in the back that was lined with cages. Most were empty – Jasmine guessed they didn't do that many operations on the weekend – but at one end, by the window, a small black-and-white shape was snuggled into a blue blanket. Jasmine peered in. The little puppy was fast asleep, but he seemed to be breathing more easily, and the horrible wound on his leg was clean and neatly stitched.

"He should be fine when he wakes up," the vet said. "He'll be sleepy for the rest of the day, though. He'll have to take some painkillers in his food for a few days, and in a week or so he'll need the stitches out, but that's all. We're not open tomorrow, but I'll be here anyway at about nine if you want to stop down and see how he is."

Jasmine nodded eagerly, and then realized that her mom and dad might not want to. She gave them a pleading look.

Her dad smiled. "It's okay, Jasmine. I'd like to know how he's doing, too. Now that we've rescued him, it feels almost like he's ours."

Jasmine smiled wistfully. If only! She would love to have a dog. But she could never be lucky enough to own a beautiful puppy like this.

Chapter Five

Vacation was meant to be fun, Molly thought miserably. You weren't supposed to spend all day holed up in your bedroom, because you were too sad even to ask a friend over. Molly just didn't think she could face any of her friends at the moment. Max had been missing since Friday, and now it was Monday. Molly wasn't giving up, of course, but her frantic searching was starting to seem hopeless. Listlessly, she heaved herself off her bed and went downstairs to find her mom.

Molly was pretty certain that her mom had given up hope of ever finding Max. She kept gently trying to point out to Molly that there had been no sign of him for three days, and no one had even mentioned seeing a puppy. But she was clearly still feeling guilty about letting him get out, so she agreed to go searching whenever Molly asked. They'd spent a couple of hours out looking every day so far, walking around town, asking people if they'd seen a little black-and-white puppy.

When Molly opened her mom's office door, her mom called her to the computer. "Look, I've been working on something for you," she said in a pleased voice.

Molly gulped. Max's face was staring at her from the screen, the word LOST shouting out at her. It was one of her favorite pictures of him – you could just tell he was wagging his tail like crazy, even though it was only his head showing. His tongue was hanging out a little, and his eyes gazed brightly into hers.

Her mom scrolled down to show her their phone number and a note saying when Max had disappeared, and asking people to check their garages and sheds in case Max had gotten shut in. "I thought we could print them out and put them up around town. I know we've asked most people already, but maybe the photo will jog people's memories."

Molly nodded, still feeling too choked

up to speak. It was so awful to think that she might only ever see Max again in pictures like this one. She couldn't think like that. But it was getting very hard not to....

"He looks great!" Jasmine gazed delightedly at the puppy bouncing around with an old chew-toy on Monday morning. He was so different from the weak little creature he'd been two days before. "His leg seems so much better."

The scary-looking cut was now just a neat line of stitches in a shaved patch of pinkish skin. Even the redness around the stitches was going away.

"He does look good, doesn't he? Puppies tend to heal pretty quickly," the vet agreed, smiling down at him. "He has a great character, really spunky. And he's a pedigree Old English sheepdog puppy, too, I think. Probably quite valuable."

Jasmine's mom was looking thoughtful. "If he's a pedigree puppy," she said, "it's not likely he was abandoned. He must have gotten lost. His owners must be really upset."

Mike nodded. "Yes, to be honest, I'm surprised we haven't heard anything. Springfield isn't that big. I would have thought that if anyone had lost a special dog like this, they'd have told the police, and it would have been passed on to us, too. He's too young to have been chipped, unfortunately." Seeing Jasmine's blank look, he explained, "Microchipped. A lot of dog owners have a tiny I.D. chip injected into their dog's neck, just in case something like this happens. It's a really good idea."

"So you haven't heard anything?" Jasmine said slowly, petting the little dog's ears. She supposed she should hope that his owners would find him, and he'd soon be back at home and safe, but she just couldn't. She'd been visiting the vet every day to see how he was – she was more interested in the puppy than in her vacation!

"No, no one's been in touch. There are a couple of other vets in the area, and I've called them, and we're going to put his picture up on our website. I think we're going to have to give him a name – I can't keep on just calling him 'puppy'!"

Jasmine smiled. "I think you should call him Lucky," she said, glad to be distracted from thinking about the puppy's real owners. "You said when we brought him in that he was lucky that the car just barely hit him, and that we found him just in time."

The vet nodded. "Mmm, that's a good idea."

The puppy looked up hopefully. He could tell they were talking about him. He liked this nice girl. She'd picked him up and carried him when he was hurt, and she kept coming to see him and play with him.

"Would you like to be called Lucky?" she said, kneeling down next to him. "Lucky? Is that a good name?"

The puppy managed a little jump up to lick her face, and barked gently, to show her he was grateful for all her petting.

"Hey, he likes it!" Jasmine said delightedly.

And so Max became Lucky....

Jasmine was quiet in the car that afternoon. They were on their way to visit some caves with underground waterfalls that her dad had found a brochure about, but she couldn't seem to feel excited about it.

"Are you all right, Jasmine?" her mom

asked. "The caves should be fun, you know. Lots of interesting stuff to see."

"I know," Jasmine said, forcing a smile.

It didn't work. "You're upset about the puppy, aren't you?" her mom said gently. "But Jasmine, you must have known the vet would try to find his owners. They'll be desperate to find him, and I'm sure he misses them, too."

"I suppose," Jasmine muttered. Actually, she couldn't help feeling that whoever had lost Lucky didn't deserve to have him, letting him run off and get hurt.

"It might even be another girl like you, Jasmine," her dad put in. "Imagine if Lucky was yours, and you'd lost him. Think how upset you'd be."

"I wouldn't have lost him!" Jasmine

burst out. "Sorry," she sniffed through her tears. "I know we can't have him, but he's so sweet, and I've always wanted a dog, and just finding him like that, it seemed so perfect…."

"And you'd been dreaming of keeping him," her mom sighed. "Oh, Jasmine, I know. He is beautiful. But he really does belong to someone else. And besides, a dog … it would be such a lot of work…." But she looked thoughtfully at Jasmine's dad as she said it.

Jasmine blew her nose firmly. "Sorry. I'm all right now. Can we go to the caves? Will there be diamonds, or anything?" she said, trying hard to sound enthusiastic. It didn't really work, but Jasmine's dad gave her mom another thoughtful look.

"Molly! Hey, Molly, wait!"

Molly and her mom turned around to see Amy running toward her, followed by Amy's older sister, Sarah. "Are you going out looking for Max again? Mom says Sarah and I can come and help, if you want."

"If that's okay," Sarah added to Molly's mom.

Molly managed a small smile. It was really sweet of Amy to want to help. "We're putting up these posters," she explained, holding one out.

Amy looked at the picture. "Oh, he looks so cute," she said sadly. "Posters are a really good idea. Are you going to put them up in the grocery store? My grandma did that when her cat was missing, and someone called her the next day to say they'd seen him."

"I hadn't thought of putting them in stores, Amy," Molly's mom said. "That's very helpful. I would think most of the store owners in town would let us."

Molly nodded hopefully. "Yes, then anyone coming in from the vacation cottages along the cliffs to do their shopping would see them."

They each took a roll of tape and walked quickly along the street, taping the posters to lampposts and fences. Molly kept having to stare into Max's beautiful big eyes as she stuck his picture up all over town.

It was so hard.

Amy put an arm around Molly's shoulders. "Hey," she said. "You never know. In a couple of days we'll probably be coming around and taking them all down because we've found him." She smiled at Molly, who wished she could feel so positive.

It was probably just natural puppy healing power that made Lucky's leg get better so quickly, but Jasmine liked to think that his new name had something to do with it. That and all the cuddles, games of hide-the-squeaky-bone, and snoozing on her lap that he'd been having. How could he not get well when everyone loved him so much?

"He really is doing so well," Mike said, shaking his head in amazement as he watched Lucky skidding across the floor after a new toy that Jasmine had brought with her on Wednesday morning, a fluffy knotted rope that had cost a considerable amount of her vacation spending money. "He'll be ready to go soon," Mike added thoughtfully. "I wouldn't have kept him for so long, except that I was hoping his owner might show up to claim him. No one's called about the photo on our website, though."

Jasmine gulped. "Go?" She faltered. "Um, go where?" Without really thinking about it, she snuggled Lucky close into her arms, and he licked her nose happily.

"To the rescue shelter. It doesn't look like we're going to have any luck finding his real owner, so Lucky is going to have to find someone new. I'd love to keep him here, but we're so busy. He needs more space and someone to take care of him properly."

A rescue shelter! It sounded awful. Jasmine knew that shelters did a wonderful job of taking care of strays and unwanted pets, but she still couldn't help thinking of them as grim, scary places. She didn't want Lucky to have to go to one of those!

"It's been great having you here to help take care of him," Mike said gratefully. "I don't know what we would have done without you." He grinned. "I'll tell you what. Friday is your last day here, isn't it?"

Jasmine nodded sadly. She didn't want to think about it. She was going to miss seeing Lucky so much!

"Well, to say thank you, how would you like to take Lucky out for his first walk? I'll bet his leg will be strong enough by then. You can take him for a walk on the beach. I gave him his puppy booster shots when you first brought him in, so he'd have less chance of picking up anything nasty from any other dogs here. He'll be fine to take out now. We can lend you a leash for him."

"Oh, I'd love to!" Jasmine hugged

Lucky tightly, and looked at her mom, her eyes shining with excitement. She imagined them wandering along the beach together, Lucky nosing into all the good-smelling holes between the rocks, as she held on to his leash.

It would be just like having her own dog....

Chapter Six

"Look, Lucky! The ocean!" Jasmine crouched down and pointed out over what seemed like miles of perfect sand to the water glinting blue in the sun. "I guess you've *probably* seen it before," she said doubtfully. "Anyway, Mom says that because the tide is out, we can walk along the shore to the next town. And there's a shop there that makes delicious milkshakes. Don't worry," she added, stroking his ears, "I'll carry you if you get tired."

Lucky wasn't really listening. He was taking deep, excited sniffs of the salty ocean air. It had an unmistakeable smell. And the last time he'd smelled it had been the day he lost Molly. Maybe he was close to her again! Wagging his tail briskly, he set off down the cliff path, with Jasmine trotting behind him, and her parents sauntering after them.

It was a gorgeous day for a walk, blue sky reflected in blue ocean, and the low tide leaving the sand firm and golden, with plenty of exciting things for a small dog to investigate.

"Ugh, Lucky, no…." Jasmine gently pushed him away from the dead crab he'd found. "It'll make you sick."

Lucky looked up at her reproachfully. But it smelled wonderful!

Jasmine ran after him, laughing, but every so often a small, cold thought would surface. *This is the last time.* They were going home tomorrow, early, and when they took Lucky back to the vet later this morning, she would have to say good-bye. Unless, of course.... Jasmine just couldn't help feeling that Mom and Dad loved Lucky, too. She saw them smiling at Lucky, who was squeaking as a wave came just a bit closer than he'd thought it would. Maybe in just a few more minutes it would be time to ask....

Molly walked slowly along the beach, a little ways behind her mom and dad. Every so often she called for Max, but there was no hope in her voice anymore. She was only doing it because if she didn't, it meant she'd given up, and that meant she was never going to see him again. At least if she was still looking, she could tell herself there was a chance.

Her dad had taken off work today so they could have a long weekend together, and he and Molly's mom tried to cheer her up by suggesting a walk along the beach to Springfield. Usually it was something she loved – it was so exciting knowing that you were racing the tide, and there were so many paths up the cliff that it wasn't really dangerous. But today, all Molly could think about was doing this walk with Max.

Molly sighed miserably. Max would have loved the beach so much. She could imagine him so easily, bounding through the sand, barking at the seagulls. Just like the little dog she could see way up the beach with another family, dragging a girl her own age along as he chased the waves. A sick, miserable tide of jealousy swept over Molly as she watched them. She blinked tears back from her eyes. The dog even *looked* like Max.

Molly sniffed determinedly and

looked away. "Max! Max!" she called hoarsely. "Here, Max, come on!"

Nothing happened. Molly wiped her arm across her eyes, and continued on after her mom and dad, staring at the stones. Maybe it was time to stop searching. She was just making herself feel worse.

Up the beach, Lucky stood listening intently, his black ears perked. He leaned forward, pulling on his leash. There were people walking along the beach, and one of them looked like Molly.

Forgetting that he was on a leash, and that his leg was still a little sore,

Lucky raced down the beach, barking excitedly, and dragging Jasmine stumbling behind him.

"Jasmine! Are you all right?" her mom called, seeing her fighting to keep up. She and Jasmine's dad hurried after them.

Molly looked up when she heard the barking, and her stomach twisted miserably. The puppy sounded just like Max, too. In fact…. Molly narrowed her eyes, and stared. It looked like Max because it *was* Max, hurling himself down the beach toward her, towing that girl.

Molly started to run, overtaking her mom and dad.

Max raced toward Molly even faster, desperate in case he lost her again. In a flurry of fur and sand, he flung himself at her, barking and wagging his tail and climbing into her lap as she knelt down to hug him.

"Max! Oh, Max! You came back! Where have you been? I can't believe I found you!" Molly gasped into his fur.

Max gave an overjoyed woof and licked the tears off her face.

"His name's Lucky," a small voice said sadly.

Molly suddenly remembered that Max was wearing a leash, and somebody else was on the other end of it. She looked up to see a blond, curly-haired girl staring down at Max.

"Or that's what we called him, anyway," the girl said, and sniffed. "I suppose he's yours, isn't he…?"

She looked like she was trying really hard not to cry, and Molly stood up slowly, cuddling Max close. "Um, yes. He climbed out the window. Exactly a week ago. My mom left it open and he got out, and we've been looking for him ever since."

"Oh." Jasmine nodded. That explained it then. "He got hit by a car," she told Lucky's real owner. "We found him. We're here on vacation."

Molly gasped in horror. "Hit by a car! Is he okay?"

Jasmine showed Molly the cut on Max's leg. "He was really lucky. The car just caught his leg, but it's healing really well. I've been visiting him every day." She sniffed again, and a tear rolled down her cheek. "I'm glad you've got him back, because he looks happy being back with you ... but I really wish we'd walked along the beach the other way!" And she turned and started stumbling away, feeling as though she couldn't bear to watch that other girl cuddling Lucky, *owning* him.

"Hey!" Molly called after her, but by this time both sets of parents had come hurrying up, and Jasmine's mom was holding her tightly. Molly saw the girl hiding her face in her mom's jacket, as everyone tried all at once to explain what was going on. Jasmine's mom took her to sit on a rock away from the others, and found some tissues, and Jasmine's dad explained how they'd found Max.

"We really can't thank you enough," Molly's dad said, shaking his head. "Max could have died."

"It was just so lucky that Jasmine found him," Molly's mom said, petting Max's head gently. "I can't believe we've got him back."

Jasmine's dad smiled. "He's a great little dog. I have to tell you, we'd pretty much decided that we were going to keep him." He looked over at Jasmine. "Jasmine doesn't know that. She took care of him so well. I think we'll have to give her a while to stop missing him, but then we'll think about getting a puppy of our own."

"Oh!" Molly gasped as a great idea hit her. "Mom! Jasmine could have Max's brother!"

"Oh, Molly, I'm not sure," her mom said doubtfully.

"There's another boy puppy in the litter Max came from," Molly explained to Jasmine's dad. "Couldn't we take them to see him?" she begged her parents. "I bet Jasmine would love him. He really looks like Max."

Jasmine's dad looked thoughtfully over at Jasmine and her mom. "I don't know. I guess we could see." He walked toward them. "Jasmine, listen, we have an idea…."

Jasmine stood in Mrs. Hughes's large kitchen, feeling miserable, and trying not to show it. She should be really excited. Lucky (she couldn't call him

Max) had found his real owners again, and wouldn't have to go to a rescue shelter. *And* her mom and dad had just told her that even though they couldn't keep Lucky, they did want to get a dog, and Lucky's brother was for sale. But Jasmine felt that it was like everyone was expecting her to adore this strange puppy right away, after she'd spent a week falling in love with Lucky.

Lucky had been left in Molly's parents' car with Molly's dad, because it might confuse him to see his brother and sisters again. The three puppies who hadn't gone to new homes yet were playing with a squishy ball, jumping all over their mom and dad, who were huge! Jasmine could see why Molly had thought of her plan – one of the puppies did look almost exactly like Lucky.

"So, what do you think, Jasmine?" her mom asked anxiously.

"Um...." Jasmine didn't know what to say. It was awful. Molly and her parents were trying to be kind, and she felt really guilty. Trying to hide how she felt, Jasmine knelt down to play with the puppies, although she didn't want to. They looked at her inquisitively, their bright eyes questioning, their ears pricking up. Jasmine couldn't help smiling a little. They were so sweet.

The boy puppy with Lucky's same pirate eye patch gave a bark. It was so clearly an invitation, or possibly even an order – *play with me!*

Jasmine giggled at the bossy little dog, and rolled the ball toward him. He yapped delightedly and pounced, flinging his paws out to make a grab for it before his sisters did.

Unfortunately the ball rolled away and he landed on his nose. He sat up and whined, not really that hurt, but embarrassed and a bit upset.

"Aw...." Jasmine picked him up and cuddled him.

The puppy snuggled into her arms, the ball forgotten as he enjoyed being cuddled. He nuzzled his nose under her chin lovingly, and Jasmine laughed as his cold, wet nose brushed her ear.

Then a sharp, shocking memory of Lucky doing just the same thing made Jasmine put the puppy down suddenly. Surprised, he whined, wanting more petting, his big eyes pleading. "Sorry, little one," Jasmine muttered, rubbing him behind the ears. I just...."

The puppy clambered into her lap and licked her cheek forgivingly. His tongue managed to be soft and rough at the same time, and Jasmine wriggled and laughed. He was tickling! Suddenly something inside her that had frozen up when Lucky raced away from her on the beach melted, and she gave Lucky's brother a big hug. Holding him tightly, she stood up carefully, and looked around at her parents.

"Do you think we could call him Lucky, too?"

Out Now:

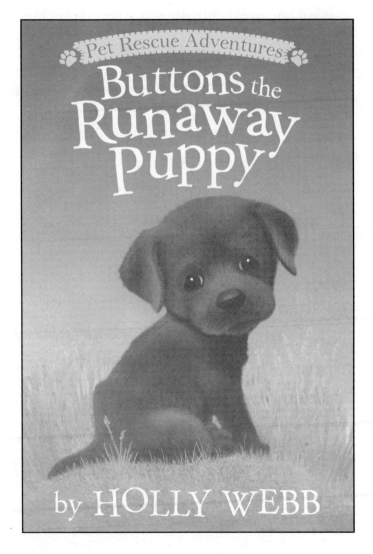

Pet Rescue Adventures

Buttons the Runaway Puppy

by HOLLY WEBB

Sophie often sees her elderly neighbor, Mr. Jenkins, walking his Labrador puppy, Buttons. Sophie loves the little dog and wishes she had one, too.

Buttons is sweet, but she's so active that she is becoming too much for Mr. Jenkins to handle. Then one day, Mr. Jenkins is injured at home, and Buttons knows she needs to find Sophie to help. Buttons gets out of the yard and takes off down the road, searching for Sophie. Will she find Sophie in time to help Mr. Jenkins?

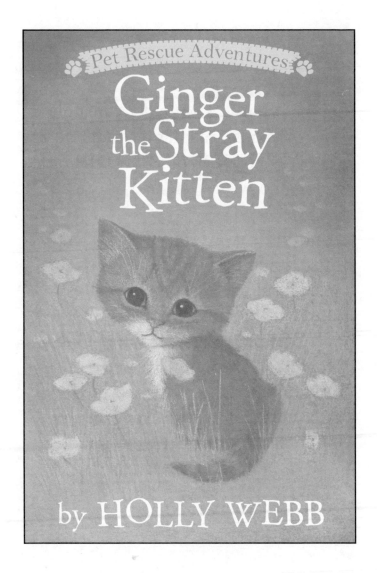

Pet Rescue Adventures

Ginger
the Stray
Kitten

by HOLLY WEBB

Rosie loves visiting the barn cats that live on the farm near her grandmother's house. Her favorite is a kitten she calls Ginger because of her beautiful orange fur.

At first, Ginger is very shy, but slowly she learns to trust Rosie. Then the farm is sold, and workers begin tearing down the buildings to put up new ones. The other cats are taken to a rescue shelter for adoption, but Ginger hides and now is all alone. Can Rosie find Ginger so she can bring the kitten home?

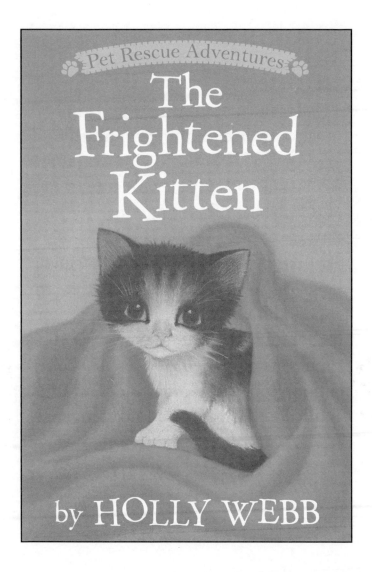

Pet Rescue Adventures

The
Frightened
Kitten

by HOLLY WEBB

Maddie loves her beautiful new tortoiseshell kitten, Cookie. She spends all her time with the kitten and can't wait until Cookie is old enough to go out in the yard.

Before long, Cookie is able to venture outside. She loves being in the yard, but there are two neighborhood cats that are always trying to chase her away. Soon, Cookie is too scared to go out and spends most of her time hiding under Maddie's bed. Can Maddie find a way to help Cookie feel brave enough to play outside again?

HOLLY WEBB

Holly Webb started out as a children's book editor, and wrote her first series for the publisher she worked for. She has been writing ever since, with more than 90 books to her name. Holly lives in England with her husband and three young sons. She has three pet cats, who are always nosing around when Holly is trying to type on her laptop.

For more information
about Holly Webb visit:

www.holly-webb.com
www.tigertalesbooks.com